The class danced the Bunny Hop one more time. By the time Brenda came back, practice was over.

"Let's return to our classroom," Mrs. Reynolds said. "We'll practice again tomorrow."

Nancy's class had just about filed into the classroom when Mrs. Reynolds gasped.

"Oh, my!" she cried.

The eggshell sculptures they had made the week before were on the floor. A box filled with colored markers had been knocked off the art shelf.

"Oh, no!" Nancy cried. "What happened to our classroom?"

The Nancy Drew Notebooks

Available from Simon & Schuster

THE
NANCY DREW
NOTEBOOKS®

#64

The Bunny-Hop Hoax

CAROLYN KEENE
ILLUSTRATED BY JAN NAIMO JONES

Aladdin Paperbacks
New York   London   Toronto   Sydney

❦ ALADDIN PAPERBACKS
An imprint of Simon & Schuster Children's Publishing Division
1230 Avenue of the Americas, New York, NY 10020
Copyright © 2005 by Simon & Schuster, Inc.
All rights reserved, including the right of reproduction in whole or in part in any form.
NANCY DREW, THE NANCY DREW NOTEBOOKS, and colophon are registered trademarks of Simon & Schuster, Inc.
The text of this book was set in Excelsior.
Manufactured in the United States of America.
10 9 8 7 6 5
First Aladdin Paperbacks edition February 2005
Library of Congress Control Number 2004114036
ISBN-13: 978-0-689-87754-4
ISBN-10: 0-689-87754-4
1111 OFF

The Bunny-Hop Hoax

1

Where's Nibbles?

We can't keep veggies forever, Bess!" eight-year-old Nancy Drew told her best friend. "They'll start to stink!"

"I don't care," Bess Marvin said. She had tears in her blue eyes. "That's all we have to remember our class pet!"

George Fayne was Bess's cousin and Nancy's other best friend. Her dark curls bounced as she shook her head.

"No it's not," George said. "We'll always remember the little hole Nibbles chewed in our dictionary!"

It was Monday morning. Nancy, Bess, and George stood in the back of the classroom with the other kids in Mrs. Reynolds's third grade class. They all stared at the bookcase where Nibbles the hamster's cage had once stood.

"I don't get it!" Andrew Leoni said. "Why would Nibbles run away?"

"Duh!" Peter DeSands said. "Because you left the cage open after you cleaned it, Andrew!"

"Oh . . . yeah." Andrew said, sighing.

Mari Chang turned to Nancy. "Why don't *you* find Nibbles, Nancy?" she asked. "Detectives always find missing things!"

Nancy loved being a detective and solving mysteries. She even had a blue detective notebook where she wrote down all her suspects and clues. But Nibbles's running away wasn't a mystery. It was an accident.

"We looked all over for Nibbles, for days," Nancy said. "Besides, it's an open and shut case."

"Yeah," Rebecca Ramirez said. "The cage was left open when it should have been shut!"

Nancy spotted the silver hamster wheel that Nibbles used to run in. She picked it up and said, "Let's keep this to remember Nibbles. He used to love it!"

She gave the wheel a spin. It made a creaky, squeaky noise.

"Maybe Nibbles liked that wheel," Brenda Carlton said, snorting. "But that creaking drove me crazy!"

Nancy rolled her eyes. Brenda was very good at writing her own newspaper, the *Carlton News*. But she wasn't very good at being nice!

"It won't creak anymore," Nancy said, "now that Nibbles is gone."

Nancy tapped the wheel over the garbage can, and a few cedar chips fell out. Then she placed it on a shelf.

"There!" Nancy declared. "Nibbles would have wanted us to have it."

Mrs. Reynolds finished writing the date on the blackboard with colored chalk. It was April 4. She told everyone to take their seats so they could start the day.

Nancy hurried to her desk. It was between the window and Bess's seat. George sat in the front near the blackboard.

"Look at the daffodils on Mrs. Reynolds's desk, Nancy," Bess whispered.

"Pretty!" Nancy said when she saw the vase filled with yellow flowers. Daffodils meant spring—and Nancy loved spring!

"I know everyone is sad about Nibbles," Mrs. Reynolds said. "But I have some very good news to cheer you all up."

Good news? Everyone whispered at once: "An extra hour of recess?" "A class trip?" "A class trip to the moon?"

"This Friday will be the Carl Sandburg Elementary School Spring Festival," Mrs. Reynolds said. "Our principal, Mrs. Oshida, wants each class to sing a song about spring, recite a poem, or dance."

Nancy's classmates grinned at one another.

"There will be a prize for the best performance," Mrs. Reynolds said. "It's a class computer program with seventy-five learning games on it."

"Seventy-five!" George said. She let out a whistle. "That's almost a hundred!"

Nancy raised her hand and asked, "What will we be doing, Mrs. Reynolds?"

"Our class will be dancing the Bunny

4

Hop," Mrs. Reynolds explained, "and it goes something like this. . . ."

The class giggled as Mrs. Reynolds began hopping forward and backward!

"And," Mrs. Reynolds continued, with a twinkle in her eye, "the dance will be led by one student, who will wear this. . . ."

Mrs. Reynolds opened the door and called, "Come on in, Orson!"

Nancy's eyes popped open as Orson Wong walked into the classroom. He was dressed in a fuzzy, white bunny costume!

"The lead bunny should be someone who has been helpful to the class," Mrs. Reynolds said. "Any suggestions?"

Brenda's hand shot up. "I wrote about the class picnic in my newspaper, the *Carlton News*," she said. "That was helpful."

"Give me a break!" Mike Minelli said. "Brenda wrote that the picnic was invaded by giant alien ants from outer space!"

Brenda stuck her chin out and said, "You all read it, didn't you?"

"I volunteered to be the closet monitor for two weeks," David Berger said.

"So you could go through everyone's

pockets for candy!" Riley McArthur said.

Mrs. Reynolds frowned. "That's it!" she said with a stern voice. "If you keep arguing, no one will be the lead bunny."

The class became very quiet. After a few seconds, Bess raised her hand.

"I elect Nancy Drew!" Bess said. "She's the best detective in our school!"

"Me?" Nancy asked. She pictured herself wearing the white bunny suit and leading the Bunny Hop. But Nancy's daydream was interrupted when the door swung open. Katie Zaleski hurried in. She was carrying a big red plastic milk crate.

"Sorry I'm late," Katie said. She put the crate down and handed Mrs. Reynolds a note. "I had to get the bunny ready."

"What bunny?" Mrs. Reynolds asked.

"This bunny!" Katie said. She lifted a little white bunny from the crate.

"Wow!" Nancy said. She brushed aside her reddish-blond bangs to get a better look. The bunny was so cute!

"My grandparents gave him to me," Katie explained, "but he doesn't get along

with my parrot, Lester. So I thought he could be our new class pet."

Mrs. Reynolds shook her head. "Rabbits can be a lot of work," she said. "What if he hops out of his crate?"

"He's never hopped out before," Katie insisted. "And all he eats is rabbit food. Like carrots, lettuce, and cabbage."

Nancy held her breath as Mrs. Reynolds thought about it. She wanted a new class pet. Especially a bunny!

"We can keep the bunny," Mrs. Reynolds said. "But only if he doesn't get into trouble."

Katie smiled as everyone cheered.

"Now we have two rabbits!" Jason Hutchings joked. "The bunny—and Orson!"

Orson's face turned red under his floppy bunny ears. "Very funny!" he said.

Mrs. Reynolds carried the crate to the back of the room. She put it on top of the bookcase where Nibbles used to be. The crate already had lots of hay and carrots and a water bottle in it.

The kids gathered around their new class pet. Bess gave the bunny some of Nibbles's celery.

"What should we name him?" Katie asked.

"Fluffy!" Bess called.

"How about Bucky?" George asked.

"I know! Carrot-breath!" Orson yelled.

"No—I have a great idea," said Riley. "I did my book report on Ben Franklin. We could name the rabbit *Bun* Franklin."

"Great idea!" Katie exclaimed.

"Okay, class, we have a *pet* bunny," Mrs. Reynolds said. "But we still need a bunny to lead the Bunny Hop."

"I elect Katie!" Nancy declared.

"Why Katie?" Brenda asked. "All she did was bring in a rabbit."

"Katie brought us our new class pet!" Nancy said. She, Bess, and George raised their hands to vote for Katie. So did most of the other kids.

"Congratulations, Katie," Mrs. Reynolds said. "You're Number One Bun!"

"No fair," Brenda mumbled.

Katie smiled as she lifted Bun Franklin out of his crate. "You hear that, Bun?" she said. "Now I'm a bunny too!"

Just then Nancy heard voices coming from the hall.

"We want to pet the bunny! We want to pet the bunny!" they shouted.

Nancy spun around. Lonny and Lenny Wong were racing into the room. They were Orson's six-year-old twin brothers. They were also double trouble!

The boys ran straight toward Katie and the bunny. Bun Franklin wiggled and wiggled until he hopped out of Katie's arms.

"Bun! Come back!" Katie cried.

Nancy and her classmates tried to catch Bun Franklin, but he was too quick. He hopped from desk to desk and from chair to chair. Then he landed on Mrs. Reynolds's desk.

Nancy gasped. The vase with the pretty daffodils fell to the floor with a big *crash*!

2

Bunny Flop

"Looks like that bunny is trouble already," Brenda said.

"No he's not!" Katie said, picking up Bun Franklin. "Those twins scared him!"

"What are you doing here anyway?" Orson asked his little brothers. "Why aren't you in your kindergarten class?"

"We were getting a drink of water," Lonny said. "And your door was open."

"We came in because we saw the bunny!" Lenny said. "We want to pet the bunny! We want to pet the bunny!"

The twins reached toward Bun Franklin.

Nancy could see that their hands were covered with paint.

"Hey!" Nancy said. "You can't touch our class pet with dirty hands!"

The twins stared at their hands.

"It's not dirt," said Lonny.

"It's finger paint!" Lenny added.

Orson marched over to his brothers and said, "Go back to your class, or I'll tell Mom!"

The twins started to giggle.

"And *we'll* tell Mom you were pretending to be a rabbit!" Lenny said.

Orson turned red again as the boys raced out of the room. "Can I take this dumb suit— I mean, rabbit suit—off now, Mrs. Reynolds?" he asked.

"Yes, Orson," Mrs. Reynolds said.

"And I'll put Bun Franklin back in his crate, Mrs. Reynolds," Katie said. "He'll be good from now on. I promise."

"I hope so," Bess whispered.

"So do I," Nancy replied. "I like having a bunny in the class."

When everyone was back in their seats,

Mrs. Reynolds gave a vocabulary quiz. Then they went over their math homework. Then the clock over the blackboard read eleven thirty, and Mrs. Reynolds exclaimed, "It's time to go outside and learn the Bunny Hop!"

"I think I'll dance in my bunny costume," Katie said. "It'll be good practice."

While Katie slipped on the rabbit suit, the others pulled on their spring jackets and coats. Nancy wore her red spring jacket. Bess had on a yellow coat with white buttons. George pulled on her gray hoodie. She didn't like clothes as much as her cousin did!

Mrs. Reynolds led the class into the school yard. Mrs. Apple's class was practicing too. They were dancing with umbrellas to a song called "Singing in the Rain."

"Should we tell them it's not raining?" Andrew whispered.

"Everyone form a line in back of Katie," Mrs. Reynolds said. Then she popped a CD into a boom box. She pressed the PLAY button, and the song began: "Do the Bunny Hop! Hop, hop, hop!"

Nancy stood behind Bess and in front of George. They put their hands on one another's shoulders.

"Kick with your right foot," Mrs. Reynolds directed. "Then with your left."

But when it was time to hop forward and backward . . .

"Watch it!" Mari cried.

"You stepped on my toe!" Riley complained.

"You hopped too fast!" David said.

"Uh-oh," Nancy whispered. "This Bunny Hop isn't as easy as I thought!"

Mrs. Reynolds played the music from the beginning again. By the third try, everyone had the steps figured out. Everyone except Katie!

"I don't get it, Mrs. Reynolds," said Katie, her bunny ears flopping. "Is it one hop or two? Do I stick out my right foot first? Or is it my left?"

"Some lead bunny!" Brenda said, scoffing.

She turned to Mrs. Reynolds and asked, "May I please get some water, Mrs. Reynolds?"

"Yes, you may, Brenda," Mrs. Reynolds said. "But when you come back, please be nicer to Katie."

Brenda nodded. She tossed her long dark hair and walked toward the school.

"Don't listen to Brenda, Katie," Nancy said. "She just wanted to wear that bunny suit."

"Over her snooty pants!" George said.

But Katie sighed and said, "Maybe Brenda's right. Maybe I shouldn't be the lead bunny. I keep messing up."

Nancy shook her head. "All you have to do is practice, Katie!" she said. "Practice makes perfect."

The class danced the Bunny Hop one more time. By the time Brenda came back, practice was over.

"Let's return to our classroom," Mrs. Reynolds said. "We'll practice again tomorrow."

Nancy's class had just about filed into the classroom when Mrs. Reynolds gasped.

"Oh, my!" she cried.

The eggshell sculptures they had made the week before were on the floor. A box filled with colored markers had been knocked off the art shelf.

"Oh, no!" Nancy cried. "What happened to our classroom?"

3

Gummy Trap

Who on earth did this?" Mrs. Reynolds asked.

Brenda pointed to a stalk of celery on the floor. "Someone left a trail of food, Mrs. Reynolds," she said. "Rabbit food!"

All eyes turned to Bun Franklin. His pink nose wiggled as he sat in the crate.

"It couldn't have been Bun," Katie argued. "He's inside his crate!"

"I'll bet he hopped out," David said.

Nancy didn't think Bun Franklin had hopped out of his crate. It was too far off the ground!

"Maybe a class rabbit isn't a good idea," Mrs. Reynolds said. "Maybe we should think of another animal."

George glanced at Brenda and muttered, "We already have a weasel."

"I heard that, George Fayne!" Brenda snapped.

Nancy wanted to help. So she studied the crate and came up with an idea.

"Why don't we flip the crate upside down?" Nancy asked. "Then there'll be no way Bun Franklin can hop out."

"There are tons of holes in the crate," George added. "So Bun Franklin can breathe and look out."

"Please, Mrs. Reynolds?" Katie asked. "Can we try it? I promise to take better care of him. I'll refill his water and celery bowl every day."

"Well," Mrs. Reynolds said. "I'll give Bun Franklin one more chance."

"Yes!" Katie cheered.

Katie hung her bunny suit in the closet, and the others put away their jackets. Suddenly Molly let out a little shriek.

"Someone just tickled my ankle!" She complained.

That's strange, thought Nancy. *No one is standing near Molly.*

"Maybe Bun Franklin did that too!" Mike said with a laugh.

Nancy quickly forgot about Molly as the class got busy flipping the crate upside down. When they were done, Katie gently slipped Bun in from the bottom.

"Let's see him try to hop out now!" Jason said as he high-fived his friends.

Nancy looked at Bun nibbling a carrot. She hadn't thought he had hopped out in the first place.

But if Bun Franklin didn't mess up the classroom, Nancy wondered, *who did?*

Nancy tried to pay attention during social studies and language arts. She made an effort to jump rope during recess. But she couldn't stop thinking about Bun Franklin.

"Even if Bun did hop out," Nancy said after school, "why would he hop back in?"

Nancy, Bess, George, and Katie were

walking home together. They swung their backpacks at their sides.

"What about the chewed-up celery on the floor?" George said. "How do you explain that?"

"Maybe someone took Bun Franklin out of his crate," Nancy said, "and put him back in after he messed up the room!"

"That's it!" Katie exclaimed. "And you're going to find out who did it, right, Nancy?"

"I am?" Nancy asked.

"Please, Nancy," Bess said. "If you don't, we might lose another class pet!"

"And who knows what our next class pet will be," George said. "A snake . . . an iguana . . . a rat . . ."

Nancy shuddered. The last thing she wanted was a creepy class pet! She pulled her detective notebook out of her backpack and said, "Let's get to work!"

The girls dropped their backpacks on the sidewalk. Nancy opened her notebook to a clean page. At the top she wrote, WHO BLAMED THE BUNNY?

"We know that our classroom was messed

up while we were dancing the Bunny Hop," Nancy said. "That means it was sometime after eleven thirty."

Nancy drew a clock in her notebook. She drew the little hand pointing to the eleven and the big hand pointing to the six.

"But who let Bun Franklin out of his crate?" Bess asked.

"Brenda was mad that she wasn't picked to lead the Bunny Hop," Nancy said. "Maybe she got Bun Franklin in trouble to make Katie look bad."

"And Brenda left Bunny-Hop practice early to get water," Bess said. "Maybe that's when she sneaked into the classroom!"

"Case closed!" Katie declared. "Brenda did it. Let's tell Mrs. Reynolds!"

Nancy shook her head. "Brenda is just a suspect so far, Katie," she said. "We have no proof that she did anything yet."

"What proof do we need?" Katie asked. "Who else could have done it?"

"Out of our way! Out of our way!" a voice yelled out.

The girls spun around. Lonny and Lenny were running down the block.

Nancy could see them stuffing candy into their mouths. They were always eating candy. The girls jumped aside as the twins raced by. The boys knocked over the girls' backpacks as they leaped over them.

"Pests," Katie muttered. "I'm never going to let them pet Bun Franklin."

Nancy's eyes lit up. "What if the twins *did* pet Bun Franklin?" she asked. "What if they sneaked into our classroom while we were practicing?"

"Write that down, Nancy," Bess said, pointing to the notebook. "Suspect number two: Lonny and Lenny!"

"Suspects two and three," George said. "There are two of them, remember?"

Nancy wrote the word SUSPECTS. Underneath she wrote BRENDA, LONNY, and LENNY. "Now, how do we find out who the real culprit is?" she asked. "Is it—"

"Ew!" Bess cut in. "There's a worm on your backpack, Nancy!"

"A worm?" Nancy gasped. She looked down and sighed with relief. "It's just a candy gummy worm one of the twins dropped."

"Brenda Carlton hates gummy worms

more than anything," Katie laughed. "Just seeing them makes her gag."

Nancy looked up from her notebook.

"If Brenda *hates* gummy worms, and the twins *love* them . . . why don't we set up a trap?"

"A trap?" George asked.

Nancy glanced around to make sure no one was listening. Then she explained.

"Whoever messed up the classroom might try to do it again. So we can put a bag of gummy worms next to Bun's crate. If the culprit returns to ruin our room again, the worms will be right there. Afterward we can look to see if any were eaten. If they were, the twins did it. If all the worms are still there, it was Brenda!"

"I like it! I like it!" George said.

"Good thinking, Nancy!" Katie said.

"I can buy the gummy worms," Bess offered excitedly. "The candy store is on my way home from school."

All four girls high-fived.

"Let's set up the trap tomorrow morning," Nancy said, "before the school bell rings."

"Why so early?" Katie asked.

"Because the early bird catches the worm," Nancy said. She picked up the sticky, gooey gummy worm. "But in this case, the worm will catch the *culprit*!"

4

Hare-Raising Trouble!

I haven't done the Bunny Hop in years, Nancy," Hannah said with a laugh.

It was late that afternoon. Nancy had gotten home from school and was in the den teaching Hannah Gruen how to do the Bunny Hop. Hannah had been the Drews' housekeeper since Nancy was three years old.

"Speaking of bunnies," Nancy said, "my class got a pet rabbit today."

"I had a pet rabbit when I was a girl," Hannah said as she hopped. "But he kept escaping from his cage."

Nancy thought of Bun Franklin and gulped. "He . . . did?" she asked.

"All the time," Hannah said. She stopped hopping. "We called him Houdini. After the famous escape artist."

Hannah went into the kitchen to check on the casserole. Nancy sat on the couch as her Labrador puppy, Chocolate Chip, padded into the den. Chip nuzzled Nancy's hand with her cool nose.

"Bun Franklin is nothing like Houdini, Chip," Nancy said. "At least I hope he's not!"

"Did you do it, Bess?" Nancy asked.

"Did you throw the gummy worms through the window?" Katie chimed in.

It was Tuesday morning in the school yard. Nancy and her friends stood whispering in a huddle.

"I tossed the bag right into the classroom," Bess said. "And you know where it landed? Next to Bun's crate!"

"Great pitch, Bess!" George said. "Especially for someone who doesn't play softball!"

Nancy grinned and said, "Now all we have to do is wait."

The girls walked through the school yard. Mrs. Reynolds was in charge that week. She had to make sure that everyone was playing safely.

As Nancy and her two friends passed Molly and Rebecca, they saw them reading copies of Brenda's newspaper, the *Carlton News*.

"Brenda's right," Molly said. "If Katie brought in a bad-news bunny, she shouldn't get to lead the Bunny Hop."

"Katie can't dance the Bunny Hop anyway," Rebecca said. "At least that's what Brenda wrote."

"Did you hear that?" Katie whispered. "Brenda is trying to get me fired!"

"Forget it, Katie," George said. "Brenda is just being . . . Brenda-ish!"

The bell rang. Mrs. Reynolds led Nancy and her classmates into the building. As they filed into their classroom, Nancy saw Bun Franklin in his crate. Then she saw Brenda at the windowsill, watering the class plants.

"Brenda was in here again!" George hissed. "She could have let Bun out of his crate!"

Nancy and her friends looked around the classroom. A plastic pencil cup had been knocked to the floor!

"Let's check out the gummy worms!" George ran to the bag of candy worms and opened it. "Eight worms in the bag. How many worms were there to start, Bess?"

"Ten," Bess said. "But—"

"Someone ate two gummy worms!" Katie said. "And that means—"

"Lonny and Lenny!" Nancy cut in.

Still wearing their jackets, Nancy, George, and Katie hurried out of the classroom and down the hall to the kindergarten wing. Bess ran after them.

"Wait!" Bess called. "I have to tell you something!"

Nancy couldn't wait. Lonny and Lenny were standing right outside their kindergarten class. They were stuffing their backpacks into their cubbies.

"Okay, you two!" Nancy called. "Did you just let our bunny out of his crate?"

"No!" Lenny said. "We still haven't even gotten to pet the bunny."

"I don't believe them!" Katie said.

The girls stood in front of the twins. Nancy put her hands on her hips.

"Where were you boys yesterday between eleven thirty and twelve?" Nancy asked.

"How should we know?" Lonny said. "We can't tell time!"

The twins dashed into the classroom and slammed the door.

"They'll never talk!" George said.

Just then Nancy saw a big piece of cardboard hanging over the cubbies. Written on it with glitter was CLASS TRIP TO THE FIREHOUSE, APRIL 4.

Nancy looked at the pictures pasted on the cardboard. They showed the kindergarten kids at the River Heights Firehouse. One shot was of Lonny and Lenny sliding down a fire pole.

"April fourth?" Nancy asked, thinking out loud. "That was yesterday."

Nancy studied the picture. "Wait a minute," she said slowly. "The twins couldn't have messed up our classroom."

"Why not?" Bess asked.

"Because they were at the firehouse when it happened," Nancy declared.

She pointed to the picture. The girls leaned closer and saw that there was a clock next to the fire pole.

"The clock says eleven thirty!" George exclaimed.

"But what about the gummy worms?" Katie asked. "If the twins didn't eat them, who did?"

"I did!" Bess blurted.

Nancy, Katie, and George whirled around. They stared at Bess.

"What?" they asked together.

"I ate two on the way to school!" Bess said. "And when I threw the bag into the classroom, I knocked over the pencil cup!"

"Give me a break, Bess!" George wailed. "Why didn't you tell us?"

"I tried to!" Bess cried.

Nancy took a deep breath. "It's okay, Bess," she said. "At least we proved that the twins are innocent."

"Girls!" Mrs. Reynolds called down the hall. "Come to class right now."

"Coming, Mrs. Reynolds!" Nancy called back. She and her friends rushed back to the classroom. After sitting down at her desk, Nancy crossed the twins' names out of her detective notebook.

Now I have only one suspect, Nancy thought. *And her name is Brenda Carlton!*

For the rest of the morning, Mrs. Reynolds's class made paper bunny ears and flower petals to wear in the Spring Festival.

After that, it was time to practice the Bunny Hop. Katie looked worried as she pulled on the bunny suit. Nancy was worried too. What if the culprit struck again during practice?

"This time I'm locking the door," Mrs. Reynolds told the class.

When they were out in the school yard, Brenda turned to Mrs. Reynolds.

"I can't dance in these shoes, Mrs. Reynolds," Brenda said. "May I clean the blackboard instead?"

"But you just watered the class plants this morning," Mrs. Reynolds said.

"I know," Brenda said with a huge smile. "I just *love* to be helpful!"

"Okay, Brenda," Mrs. Reynolds said. She handed her the classroom key. "But tomorrow wear comfortable shoes."

"Thank you, Mrs. Reynolds!" Brenda turned and ran toward the building.

"Some tight shoes," George said. "She practically skipped all the way inside!"

Nancy kept wondering—was Brenda up to something?

The kids lined up behind Katie. The music started, and Katie hopped too fast and fell on the ground!

"Yeah, I know." Katie groaned as she stood up. "Practice makes perfect."

Suddenly Brenda ran out of the building. "Mrs. Reynolds, Mrs. Reynolds! Something happened inside. Come quick!"

The class raced into the classroom. Nancy stared at the paper bunny ears and flower petals on the floor. Some were crumpled, and Mrs. Reynolds's water bottle had spilled all over the floor.

"It was like this when I came in, Mrs. Reynolds!" Brenda said. She picked up another chewed-up celery stalk. "I guess the bunny went bonkers again."

Nancy looked at Bun Franklin. He was sitting quietly in his upside-down crate. But the bowl of celery was knocked over.

"Or maybe," Nancy said, "somebody let the bunny out of his crate!"

5

Chew Clue

Or maybe," Kyle said with a grin, "Bun Franklin lifted the crate all by himself. Maybe he's Super Bunny!"

The boys and girls laughed nervously. But Nancy didn't. If only she could tell Mrs. Reynolds what she thought about Brenda. But she still had no proof!

"Don't send Bun Franklin home yet, Mrs. Reynolds," Katie pleaded. "I'll bring in a brand new rabbit cage tomorrow. With a door and a latch and everything!"

Mrs. Reynolds thought a new cage was a good idea. So she gave Bun Franklin one final chance.

While the kids picked up the paper bunny ears and flower petals, Bess found something else on the floor. It was her favorite pencil. The one with the white eraser shaped like a unicorn.

"Phooey!" Bess said. "Bun Franklin chewed up my pencil when he was running around. It's got teeth marks all over it."

"Sorry," Katie said.

"It's not Bun Franklin's fault," Nancy said. "He was just being a bunny."

Nancy searched for clues around Bun Franklin's crate. The only thing she noticed was that one celery stalk was gone.

"I wish you could talk, Bun Franklin," Nancy whispered. "Then you could tell me if Brenda really did it!"

"How many bunnies are at the Cottontail Bunny Ranch?" Nancy asked.

"I think there are seventy-five of them," Katie answered.

"Why so many?" Bess asked.

Mrs. Zaleski smiled as she drove the blue minivan. "Because they multiply!" she called over her shoulder.

"Cool!" George said. "Maybe they can help me with my math homework!"

It was four o'clock in the afternoon. Katie had invited Nancy, Bess, and George to the Cottontail Bunny Ranch. That was where Mrs. Zaleski was going to buy Bun Franklin's brand-new cage!

"Here we are, girls," Mrs. Zaleski said as she drove through the ranch gate. "The Cottontail Bunny Ranch!"

A man dressed in blue jeans and a matching jacket came to greet them.

"Girls, this is Mr. Harewood," Mrs. Zaleski said as they climbed out of the minivan. "He owns the ranch."

Mr. Harewood grinned with big white teeth—just like a bunny's!

"If I'd known you were coming," Mr. Harewood said, "I would have given you a Twenty-One-*Bun*-Salute!"

"Bunny jokes," George whispered. "I'll bet he's got a million of them."

"We're here to buy a new cage for Katie's rabbit," Mrs. Zaleski explained.

"You mean a new *hutch*," Mr. Harewood explained. "That's where rabbits live."

"Hutch," Nancy repeated.

"A good hutch is big enough for a rabbit to hop around in," Mr. Harewood explained. "It has a built-in water bottle, litter tray, and food dish."

"Does it have a door with a lock on it?" Nancy asked. "A good strong lock?"

"How about an alarm?" George asked. "In case somebody sneaky opens the door?"

"And a built-in camera?" Katie added. "So we can catch that sneak in the act?"

Mr. Harewood blinked a few times. "Are you sure you girls want a rabbit hutch?" he asked.

"A simple hutch will do," Mrs. Zaleski said, smiling. "May I see a few?"

"And can we see the bunnies?" Bess asked, jumping up and down. "Please?"

"Bunnies?" Mr. Harewood boomed. "What are we waiting for? Let's get hoppin'!"

While Mrs. Zaleski looked at hutches, Mr. Harewood led the girls through the bunny ranch. Most of the bunnies were hopping around inside big wired pens. Mr. Harewood opened a gate so the girls could step inside.

"Be very gentle," Mr. Harewood said as he handed each girl a bunny.

Nancy giggled as her little white bunny wiggled in her arms. "This one looks just like Bun Franklin!" she said.

"How do you like your new pet rabbit?" Mr. Harewood asked.

"We like him!" Bess said. "Except that today he chewed up my favorite pencil."

Bess placed her bunny on the ground. She pulled the pencil out of her jacket pocket and showed it to Mr. Harewood.

"Hmm," Mr. Harewood said. "Are you sure a bunny did this?"

"Pretty sure," Bess said. "Why?"

"Well," Mr. Harewood said. "Because—"

"Oh, Mr. Harewood!" Mrs. Zaleski called. "I think I found my hutch."

"*Bun*-tastic!" Mr. Harewood called back. He tossed the pencil to Bess. "Excuse me, girls. Got to get hoppin'."

The girls all stared at Mr. Harewood as he walked away.

"Maybe he doesn't think they're bunny teeth marks," Bess said.

"And if anyone knows bunnies," Katie said, "it's Mr. Harewood."

But Nancy wanted to see for herself. She placed her bunny on the ground and looked around the pen. A small brown rabbit was chewing on a piece of wood.

"Let's compare teeth marks," Nancy said.

The brown bunny hopped away as the girls walked over. Bess, George, and Katie watched as Nancy held the two sets of teeth marks side by side.

"Hmm," Nancy said. "The teeth marks on the pencil are a lot smaller than the ones on the wood."

"So Bun Franklin couldn't have chewed up the pencil!" Katie said.

"Then who did?" George asked.

Nancy studied the pencil. "These teeth marks are even too tiny to be human," she said. "Way too tiny."

The girls became very quiet. Until Bess exclaimed, "Well, *somebody* chewed up my unicorn pencil!"

"Somebody," Nancy said slowly, "or *something*!"

6

Bye-Bye, Bunny

"Are you sleepy, Pudding Pie?" Mr. Drew asked Nancy.

"Sleepy?" Nancy asked with a yawn. "What makes you say that, Daddy?"

"Because you just poured orange juice over your cereal," Mr. Drew answered.

Nancy gulped. Her father was right. It was Wednesday morning and she had hardly slept the night before.

"I guess I am sleepy, Daddy," Nancy said. "I was reading late last night."

Hannah leaned over Nancy's shoulder to pour her a new bowl of cereal. "Your schoolbook?" she asked.

"No," Nancy said, shaking her head. "My detective notebook!"

Nancy told her father all about Bun Franklin. Mr. Drew was a lawyer, and he liked helping Nancy with her cases. He had even given Nancy her blue detective notebook.

"So far my only suspect is Brenda," Nancy said. "But I have no proof that she did it. And my only clues are those weird teeth marks on Bess's pencil."

Nancy showed her father a page in her notebook. She had drawn little dashes the same size as the teeth marks.

Mr. Drew tapped the tip of Nancy's nose and smiled. "Sometimes no clues can be a clue too," he said. "Think about it."

Nancy tried to. But it didn't make sense. How could no clues be a clue?

"I hope you're right," Nancy sighed. "Because right now, I'm totally clueless!"

Nancy finished her cereal. She brushed her reddish-blond hair, put on her denim jacket, and hurried off to school.

As soon as Nancy walked into the class-room with her friends, she saw Bun

Franklin. He was already inside his brand-new hutch.

"My mom brought it in before school started," Katie said. "Doesn't Bun look happy?"

"You mean *hoppy*!" George joked.

"Now you sound like Mr. Harewood!" Katie groaned.

Nancy glanced at Brenda. She was over by the closet, admiring Katie's bunny suit.

"Do the Bunny Hop," Brenda was singing softly. "Hop, hop, hop."

Nancy kept a close eye on Brenda during math, current events, and science. When she watched Brenda during recess, she didn't like what she saw.

"This is called a petition," Brenda said, waving a piece of paper. "If enough of you sign it, the lead bunny job will be taken away from Katie."

Nancy was glad Katie was on the other side of the school yard. She was practicing the Bunny Hop with Mrs. Reynolds.

"That's mean, Brenda," Nancy said. "Why would we want to sign that?"

"I know Katie is your friend, Nancy,"

Brenda said. "But you have to think of the Bunny Hop. You don't want our class to lose on Friday, do you?"

Nancy folded her arms across her chest. "I'd rather lose than be mean."

"Me too!" George said.

"Me three!" Bess said.

Brenda narrowed her eyes. But then she forced a smile. "Everyone knows that I'm the best person to lead the Bunny Hop!" she said. "I'm a great dancer—"

Brenda did a little dance step.

"And I'm very helpful," Brenda added. "I watered the plants and cleaned the blackboard!"

"And let Bun Franklin out of his cage," Bess murmured.

"What?" Brenda demanded.

"Nothing," Bess said coolly.

Brenda flipped her hair and walked away. Nancy narrowed her eyes and said, "That proves something."

"What does it prove?" George asked.

"That Brenda wants Katie's job so badly, she'll do anything to get it," Nancy said. "Like starting that mean petition!"

The bell rang and recess was over. The kids filed back inside the classroom. Suddenly Jason stopped in his tracks and pointed at the blackboard.

"Cheese and crackers!" he cried.

Nancy gasped. This time all of the chalk had been knocked off the blackboard. And another stalk of celery lay on the floor!

"Bun couldn't have done it!" Katie wailed. "His new hutch has a lock!"

Nancy glanced at Brenda. She couldn't have let Bun Franklin out either. She'd stayed in the school yard during recess!

What if Bun Franklin really is escaping? Nancy wondered. *What if he is like Hannah's rabbit, Houdini? Or what if he really is . . . Super Bunny?*

"I don't like our new class pet," Rebecca said.

"Me neither," Jason said.

"I hate to say this, Katie," Mrs. Reynolds said. "But I think you should take Bun Franklin home. At least until we find out who's been messing up our room."

"I can't!" Katie cried. "My parrot, Lester, doesn't like bunnies!"

"Maybe someone else can take Bun Franklin home," Mrs. Reynolds said. "Until he has a new place to live."

"I already have a dog," Mari said.

"I have a cat," Peter said.

"I have two little brothers," Orson grumbled.

"What about you, Nancy?" Katie asked eagerly. "You like Bun Franklin!"

Nancy gulped. What if Bun escaped from his hutch and messed up her house?

"I'll have to ask my father first," Nancy said. "And Hannah—"

"You can call them from the school office during lunch," Mrs. Reynolds said.

"I'm sure they'll say yes," Katie said excitedly. "Thanks, Nancy."

Nancy smiled. Maybe having a bunny for a few days would be fun. She reached into the hutch and gently pulled Bun Franklin out. Pieces of hay fell from his feet onto the floor.

"Bun always has hay stuck on his feet," Katie said. "You should have seen my room after Lester chased him."

Nancy stared at Bun Franklin's feet. If he had been running around the classroom, wouldn't he have left hay all over it too?

So that's what Daddy meant when he said no clues could be a clue too!

Nancy placed Bun back in his hutch. As they tidied up the classroom, Nancy whispered to her friends, "I don't think *anybody* took Bun Franklin out of his hutch. I think somebody is messing up our classroom on his or her own!"

"Why would somebody do that?" George whispered.

"And what if he or she comes back?" Bess squeaked.

"If only we could hide a secret video camera in the classroom," Nancy said. "Or a tape recorder."

Katie smiled and said, "I have something *better* than a tape recorder."

"What is it?" Nancy asked.

"It's a surprise," Katie whispered. "You'll see what I mean tomorrow morning!"

At lunch, Nancy ate her egg-salad sandwich and drank her grape juice. Then she hurried to the school office to call her father and Hannah.

Nancy got permission to take Bun Franklin

home. At three o'clock, Hannah drove to school to pick up Nancy and Bun Franklin.

Hannah knew how to set up the hutch in the Drews' basement. She also knew what food rabbits liked to eat.

"Fresh celery for Bun Franklin!" Hannah said as she slipped the green stalk through the bars. "*Bun* appétit!"

Bun Franklin sniffed at the celery. Then he hopped to the corner of his hutch.

"Maybe he's not hungry," Nancy said.

But then Bun hopped over to a leaf of lettuce and chewed it hungrily.

"I guess Bun Franklin doesn't like celery!" Hannah said.

"Huh?" Nancy asked. She thought about all the chewed-up celery stalks on the classroom floor.

"Now I know that Bun Franklin never left his cage, Hannah!" Nancy said. "He doesn't even like celery!"

7

Hide and Creak

T a-daaa!" Katic sang. "Meet our new class pet of the day!"

It was Thursday morning. Katie had just walked into the classroom with her pet parrot, Lester, perched on her shoulder.

"I don't know," Mrs. Reynolds said. "We've never had a class pet for the day—"

"Arrrk!" Lester screeched. "Pretty lady! Pretty lady! Arrrk!"

Mrs. Reynolds smiled. "I suppose Lester can stay for the day," she said.

"Awesome!" Katie said. "He doesn't need a cage. Just something to perch on."

The kids followed Katie to the back of the room. As they walked, Katie spoke to Nancy, Bess, and George out of the corner of her mouth.

"Parrots repeat what they hear," Katie murmured. "Just like a tape recorder. Get it?"

"I get it!" Nancy said. "So if the creep comes back to mess up our classroom, Lester will tell us what he heard!"

"Creep! Creep!" Lester squawked.

"Who's he calling a creep?" Jason demanded.

"Chill out," Katie sighed. She carefully perched Lester on the easel.

"Chill, chill! Raak!"

"By the way, Nancy," Katie said. "My mom said she'd take Bun Franklin to the Cottontail Bunny Ranch today. So you don't have to keep him at your house anymore."

"Oh," Nancy said. She was just starting to like having a pet bunny.

Nancy's thoughts were interrupted by Brenda's voice.

"Mrs. Reynolds?" Brenda asked. "I have a

petition I'd like to show you. It's about Katie and the Bunny Hop!"

"What petition?" Katie asked.

"I don't believe it!" George whispered to Nancy. "Miss Snooty Pants is still trying to be the lead bunny!"

"Snooty Pants!" Lester squawked loudly. "Snooty Pants! Raaak!"

Brenda glared at Lester. "Put a sock in it, cracker-breath!" she shouted.

"That wasn't nice, Brenda!" Mrs. Reynolds scolded. "And neither is a petition against someone in your class."

Brenda plopped down in her seat and folded her arms.

Good, Nancy thought. *Now Brenda's petition against Katie will never work.*

When everyone was seated, Mrs. Reynolds spoke about the Spring Festival. She told everyone to come in the next morning bright and early, at eight o'clock. Next she told everyone to wear colorful and comfy clothes.

"And now we'll have our very last Bunny-Hop practice," Mrs. Reynolds said.

"Bye, Lester!" Nancy said softly as they

left the classroom. "I hope you're all ears. And beak!"

Outside in the schoolyard a fourth grade class was practicing too. It was Mr. Kaplan's class, dancing around a maypole.

"I heard they built it all by themselves," Brenda groaned. "We're going to lose!"

During practice Katie kicked her right foot when it should have been her left. She hopped forward when she should have hopped backward.

"Practice at home tonight, Katie," Mrs. Reynolds said when practice was over. "Yes, Mrs. Reynolds." Katie sighed.

But as the class walked inside, Katie turned to Nancy, Bess, and George. "I think I'm going to quit leading the Bunny Hop," she said.

"Why?" Nancy asked.

"I only got the job because I brought in Bun Franklin," Katie said. "And that didn't even work out. Maybe Brenda should be the lead bunny."

"Don't, Katie!" Bess said.

"Now Miss Snooty Pants will get her

way!" George said. "And she always—"

"Hey!" Kyle's voice cut in. "Who ate my Gooey Chewy bar?"

Everyone stared at Kyle. He was pulling a candy bar out of his jacket pocket. The top part of the wrapper was shredded. A chunk of candy had been bitten off.

"My jacket was in the closet all morning!" Kyle said. "So who ate it?"

"Don't blame Bun Franklin," Katie said. "He's not here anymore."

"And don't blame me," David added. "I haven't been the closet monitor for weeks!"

This is too weird, Nancy thought. *But so is everything else lately!*

Nancy and her classmates walked inside the building, then into their room.

"Oh, no!" Mrs. Reynolds cried. "Not again!"

The pencil sharpener on Mrs. Reynolds's desk had been knocked down. A pile of pencil shavings lay on the floor.

"Raaak!" a voice squawked.

"Lester!" Nancy remembered. She and her friends hurried over to the parrot.

"Okay, Lester," Nancy said, "tell us what you heard. Every word!"

Lester blinked. He stretched his neck and squawked, "Creak . . . creak!"

"'Creak?'" George asked. "What's he talking about?"

"Lester probably heard something that creaks," Katie said with a shrug.

"The only thing that creaks is Nibbles's old hamster wheel," Nancy said.

Suddenly it clicked!

"Nibbles!" Nancy said to herself. "Chewed-up celery . . . tiny teeth marks . . . that's it!"

Nancy ran to grab the hamster wheel. She examined it closely. Inside the wheel were small pieces of green stuff.

Celery! Nancy thought.

"The wheel was clean when I put it away," Nancy said. "Now look at it!"

The others had gathered in the back to listen.

"Bun Franklin doesn't eat celery," Nancy went on. "But Nibbles did. He also loved running around in his wheel. And he had teeny-tiny teeth too!"

"Nancy?" Mrs. Reynolds asked slowly. "What are you saying?"

Nancy smiled at Mrs. Reynolds and said, "I'm saying that I think I know who's been messing up our classroom!"

8

Spring Surprise

Go ahead, Nancy," Mrs. Reynolds urged. "Tell us who did it."

"It was Nibbles!" Nancy declared.

"Nibbles?" the kids cried together.

Nancy told the class what she knew. She could see the kids getting excited.

"So that's who ate my candy bar!" Kyle laughed.

"And tickled my ankle!" Molly said.

"Let's look for Nibbles again!" Rebecca said. "Maybe he's still hiding!"

The kids walked around the classroom calling the hamster's name.

"Nibbles!" Nancy called. "Come out, come out, wherever you are!"

They looked behind books, inside desks, and even in the class garbage can.

Nancy opened the closet door and peeked inside. "Nibbles!" she called. "Are you in there?"

George crawled inside the closet on her hands and knees. "No hamster in here!" she shouted.

"Go back to your seats, boys and girls," Mrs. Reynolds said. "We can't look for Nibbles all day."

"Especially when he's not here." Brenda sniffed.

"I knew it was too good to be true." Rebecca sighed. "Nibbles is gone forever."

Nancy, Bess, George and Katie walked slowly back to their desks.

"I'm pretty sure it was Nibbles," Nancy said. "But how can I prove it if we can't find him?"

Katie was still wearing the bunny suit. She walked past her desk.

"Where are you going?" Bess asked.

"To tell Mrs. Reynolds I'm quitting being lead bunny," Katie said.

Nancy, Bess, and George watched as Katie spoke quietly to Mrs. Reynolds. Mrs. Reynolds then called Brenda to the front of the classroom. The three of them spoke together until—

"Yes!" Brenda cheered. She began jumping up and down. "I'm Number One Bun!"

Nancy felt bad for Katie. But she felt bad for herself, too.

This case will never be solved, Nancy thought. *Not until I find Nibbles!*

"Wow!" George cried. "Do you believe this is our school yard?"

"It's so . . . springy!" Nancy said.

Nancy and Bess were wearing hats decorated with paper flower petals around their heads. George had on pink paper bunny ears. It was Friday, the day of the Spring Festival!

An arch of yellow, white, and purple balloons curved over the school yard. Huge cardboard flowers were pasted on the brick walls of the school.

Mrs. Reynolds's students stood in line. They were so excited, they could hardly stand still!

Brenda was dressed in the fuzzy, white bunny costume. Pinned on it was a button that read, SUPERSTAR.

"This is it, you guys!" Brenda said. "Think of those seventy-five computer games, and don't blow it!"

Mrs. Oshida, the school principal, welcomed everyone to the festival. Then she introduced the first class: Mrs. Fox's kindergarten.

The kindergartners held flowers and sang "The Lazy Daisy." Lenny sniffed his flowers and began to sneeze.

Nancy tried to pay attention, but she couldn't stop thinking about Nibbles.

I know Nibbles messed up the classroom, Nancy thought. *So why can't we find him?*

The first and second graders performed. Then it was time for the third grade. Mrs. Apple's class danced to "Singing in the Rain." One girl's umbrella got stuck as she tried to open it.

"Are we lucky or what?" Brenda said. "Now we have a better chance to win!"

64

When Mrs. Apple's class was finished, Mrs. Oshida said, "Mrs. Reynolds's class will now dance the Bunny Hop."

"That's us!" Nancy said.

"Remember," Mrs. Reynolds told them. "The most important thing is to have fun."

"And to win," Brenda said as they marched to the middle of the school yard. "Keep thinking about those seventy-five games, you guys!"

"Since when is she the boss of us?" George whispered.

"Since she became Number One Bun," Bess whispered back.

Everyone lined up behind Brenda. Nancy stood right behind her, and Bess and George were right behind Nancy. Katie chose to stand all the way in the back.

The class waited quietly until Mrs. Reynolds started the music. Then they began the dance.

Right foot, left foot, Nancy thought. *Hop, hop, hop!*

Suddenly Brenda stopped short. Everyone shouted as they bumped into each other.

"Hey!" Orson complained. "What's with the traffic jam?"

Brenda ran out of the line. She began jumping up and down and shaking.

"Eek! Eek!" Brenda cried. "Get it out! Get it out!"

Mrs. Reynolds rushed over. "Get what out, Brenda?" she asked.

"Something is in my pocket!" Brenda cried. "I can feel it moving!"

Nancy looked at the pocket on the side of the bunny suit. A little brown furry head popped out of it!

"A mouse!" Brenda shouted. The creature jumped out of the pocket. Then it scurried into a crowd of teachers. Mrs. Fox shrieked as it darted around her legs.

Nancy couldn't take her eyes off the little creature. It wasn't a mouse at all. "Nibbles!" Nancy cried.

Nancy ran to pick up the hamster. She held him up for everyone to see. Her classmates looked glad to see their class pet. But they also looked confused.

"How did Nibbles get inside the bunny suit?" Mari asked.

Nancy put the pieces together.

"He must have crawled into the pocket while it was hanging in the closet last night," Nancy explained. "He had nowhere to go since we put away his cage."

"Why didn't Nibbles come out when we were in the classroom?" Molly asked.

"Nibbles was probably scared to be out of his cage," Nancy said. "And hungry and thirsty. That's why he drank from Mrs. Reynolds's water bottle. And ate the celery."

"And my Gooey Chewy bar!" Kyle said.

"I think we owe Katie an apology," Mrs. Reynolds said. "Bun Franklin never messed up our room."

"Apology accepted," Katie said with a smile. "Now let's dance the Bunny Hop!"

"No way!" Brenda said. She peeled off the bunny suit and stepped out of it. "I'm not wearing this icky suit. Not after that rat was in it!"

"Hamster," Nancy corrected.

"Why don't we let Nancy lead the Bunny Hop?" Bess asked. "She solved the mystery for us!"

Nancy grinned. Leading the Bunny Hop

would be an honor—and a lot of fun!

"What do you say, Nancy?" Mrs. Reynolds asked.

"I say—let's get hoppin'!" Nancy answered. She handed Nibbles gently to Mrs. Reynolds. Then she put on the bunny suit.

"You'll make a good lead bunny, Nancy," Brenda said.

"Thanks, Brenda!" Nancy asked.

"Sure," Brenda said. She reached out and yanked the superstar button off the suit. "But this belongs to me."

Everyone lined up behind Nancy. They waited until the music played. Then they began to dance!

Right foot, left foot, Nancy thought. *Hop, hop, hop!*

Nancy and her classmates did their best. When the festival was over, the fourth grade won first prize for their maypole dance. Mrs. Apple's class won second prize for "Singing in the Rain."

"Whoever heard of a maypole in April?" Brenda complained.

"And it's not even raining!" Andrew said again.

But Nancy and her classmates had tons to be happy about. And that night in her bedroom, Nancy had tons to write in her detective notebook:

I guess practice really does make perfect. We won third prize in the Spring Festival—and a whole set of neon paints for our easel!

But there's a lot more to cheer about. First, I solved the case. Second, we finally found Nibbles. And third, Bun Franklin has a great home at the Cottontail Bunny Ranch! Bun will like it there. He'll have other bunnies to play with, lots of carrots, and plenty of bunny jokes too. It'll be a fresh new start. Just like spring!

CASE CLOSED!

Become Nancy Drew to Solve a 3D Interactive Mystery!

Danger and Intrigue Await You in Eleven Exciting Adventures

For Mystery Fans 10 and up

For more information visit
www.nancydrewgames.com.

Order on-line at www.herinteractive.com
or call 1-800-461-8787.

WINDOW 98/2000/Me/XP

Created by

Distributed by

Secrets Can Kill
Read between the lines as super-sleuth
Nancy Drew to expose a killer!

Stay Tuned for Danger
Go undercover to save daytime TV's biggest
star from the danger lurking in the wings.

Message in a Haunted Mansion
Discover who—or what—is behind the
mysterious accidents in a house of secrets.

Treasure in the Royal Tower
Follow ancient clues to expose a castle's
legendary secret.

The Final Scene
Search a darkened movie theater to free a
hostage from her captor's dangerous plot.

Secret of the Scarlet Hand
Expose buried secrets as super-sleuth
Nancy Drew and catch a thief red-handed!

Ghost Dogs of Moon Lake
Hunt for clues as super-sleuth Nancy Drew
on the trail of a pack of phantom hounds!

The Haunted Carousel
Take a spin with danger to unravel the
mystery of a ghostly merry-go-round!

Danger on Deception Island
Plunge into danger to bring a mysterious
island's secrets to the surface!

The Secret of Shadow Ranch
Take a wild ride into terror and trickery to
rein in a ghostly secret!

Curse of Blackmoor Manor
Journey to the moors of England to reveal
a family secret long hidden in the fog!

She's sharp.

She's smart.

She's confident.

She's unstoppable.

And she's on your trail.